WAKE UP, BLACK BEAR!

by Dawn Bentley

Illustrated by Beth Stover

Little® Soundprints

For Tyler William Bentley—

"A long time ago, there was a fish in a lake and some people say that fish never came out of the lake. The end."

Even your "scary" stories make me laugh! I am blessed to have a nephew as special as you. I love you. — D.B.

Published by Soundprints Division of Trudy Corporation, Norwalk, Connecticut.

Book design: Marcin D. Pilchowski
Editor: Laura Gates Galvin
Editorial assistance: Chelsea Shriver

First Edition 2003
10 9 8 7 6 5 4 3
Printed in China

Acknowledgments:
   Our very special thanks to Dr. Don E. Wilson of the Department of Systematic Biology at the Smithsonian Institution's National Museum of Natural History for his curatorial review.
   Soundprints would also like to thank Ellen Nanney and Robyn Bissette at the Smithsonian Institution's Office of Product Development and Licensing for their help in the creation of this book.
   Many thanks to Laura Gates Galvin, my editor-extraordinaire, who made this project a joy to work on! (D.B.)

Library of Congress Cataloging-in-Publication Data

Bentley, Dawn.
   Wake up, Black Bear! / by Dawn Bentley ; illustrated by Beth Stover.
      p. cm.
   Summary: After a winter of sleeping, Black Bear and her cubs catch fish, eat honey, and climb trees in the spring sunshine.
      ISBN 1-59249-007-7 (pbk.)
      1. Black bear—Juvenile fiction. [1. Black bear—Fiction. 2. Bears—Fiction.]
   I. Stover, Beth, 1969- ill. II. Title.

PZ10.3.B4517 Wak 2003
[E]—dc21
                                                                    2002191156

Table of Contents

A note to the reader:
Throughout this story you will see words in **bold letters**. There is more information about these words in the glossary. The glossary is in the back of the book.

Chapter 1

Wake Up, Sleepyheads

Black Bear is sleeping in her **den**. Black Bear has two **cubs**. They are sleeping, too.

The tiny cubs have no hair or teeth. Black Bear cuddles the cubs to keep them warm.

Three months later,

Black Bear wakes up.

The cubs wake up, too.

Spring is here!

Black Bear leaves
the den. The cubs
follow Black Bear.
The cubs want to
explore the forest.

Chapter 2

Exploring the Forest

The cubs sniff the air. The cubs listen to new sounds. There is so much to see and do.

Black Bear watches the cubs play. The cubs chase each other up and down trees.

Black Bear drinks from a stream. A beaver in the stream sees Black Bear. The beaver is scared. He quickly swims home.

Black Bear is hungry. Black Bear sees a **trout** in the stream. Black Bear catches the trout.

The cubs chase a frog. The frog gets away. Soon the cubs will be better hunters.

Chapter 3

Treats to Eat

Black Bear hears bees.

Black Bear sees bees.

Where there are bees,

there is honey. Black

Bear loves honey!

Black Bear finds the honey. The cubs eat the honey. Now the cubs love honey, too!

Black Bear is tired.

She wants to rest.

The cubs are not

tired. They want

to play.

The cubs pull and
tug on Black Bear.
Black Bear growls.
The cubs will let
Black Bear rest.

The cubs climb
a tree. They hang
from their paws.
They jump from
the branches.

Black Bear knows her cubs will not get hurt. They are good climbers and are safe in the trees.

Chapter 4

Back to Sleep

The bears spend
the spring eating.
The bears spend
the summer eating.
The bears spend
the fall eating.

The cubs are
now big and fat.
Black Bear is big
and fat, too. Soon
it will be winter.

The bears will sleep for the winter. Black Bear finds a cave. The cave is dark and dry.

The bears will sleep in the cave. Black Bear cuddles her cubs. They begin their long winter nap again.

Glossary

Den: an animal's shelter.

Cub: a baby bear.

Trout: a fish with sharp teeth found in streams and lakes.

Wilderness Facts
About the Black Bear

Black bears can be found in the forests of North America and Canada. Black bears are not always black. They can be black, blonde, red or dark brown.

Black bears eat a lot to prepare for hibernation. Bears hibernate during the winter. They don't eat when they are hibernating. They live off the fat stored in their bodies. During hibernation, black bears lose 20 to 40 percent of their body weight.

Black bears have long, sharp claws. Their claws help them climb trees. Bears also use their claws to defend themselves against predators.

Animals that live near black bears in the Atlantic wilderness include:

Beavers

Eastern chipmunks

Eastern gray squirrels

Fishers

Little brown bats

Moose

Porcupines

Raccoons

Red foxes

Striped skunks

White-tailed deer

Wood frogs